Michael Gruenbaum was born in Prague, Czechoslovakia. He survived the Holocaust and recently wrote about his teenage life during World War ll in a book entitled *Somewhere There Is Still a Sun*. The book was published by Simon and Schuster which has already sold some 80,000 copies; the book has also already been translated into 16 languages. After getting his BSCE in civil engineering from MIT and his MCP from Yale University, he had an illustrious career for many decades in the traffic and transportation planning field in the Boston area, during which time he authored the pioneering book, *Transportation Facts for the Boston Region*.

Thelma Gruenbaum was Michael's wife for 50 years until she succumbed to ALS in 2006. She was born in Springfield, Illinois, and attended the University of Chicago for seven years for her undergraduate as well as graduate work toward a Ph.D. in Human Development. She was the author of several books, *Before 1776: The Massachusetts Bay Colony from Founding to Revolution, To Music and Children with Love, Reflections for Parents and Teachers*, and *Nesarim: Child Survivors of Terezin*. Thelma and Michael have three children and four grandchildren.

Tell Me About Beethoven

MICHAEL AND THELMA GRUENBAUM

Austin Macauley Publishers™
LONDON • CAMBRIDGE • NEW YORK • SHARJAH

Copyright © Michael Gruenbaum and Thelma Gruenbaum 2022

All rights reserved. No part of this publication may be reproduced, distributed, or transmitted in any form or by any means, including photocopying, recording, or other electronic or mechanical methods, without the prior written permission of the publisher, except in the case of brief quotations embodied in critical reviews and certain other non-commercial uses permitted by copyright law. For permission requests, write to the publisher.

Any person who commits any unauthorized act in relation to this publication may be liable to criminal prosecution and civil claims for damages.

Ordering Information
Quantity sales: Special discounts are available on quantity purchases by corporations, associations, and others. For details, contact the publisher at the address below.

Publisher's Cataloging-in-Publication data
Gruenbaum, Michael and Gruenbaum, Thelma
Tell Me About Beethoven

ISBN 9781649794604 (Paperback)
ISBN 9781649794598 (Hardback)
ISBN 9781649794611 (ePub e-book)

Library of Congress Control Number: 2021947829

www.austinmacauley.com/us

First Published 2022
Austin Macauley Publishers LLC
40 Wall Street, 33rd Floor, Suite 3302
New York, NY 10005
USA

mail-usa@austinmacauley.com
+1 (646) 512 5767

To our sons: David, Peter and Leon Gruenbaum.

And to the Writers' Group of Brookline, MA, a group consisting of: Ina Friedman, Natalie Rothstein, Roberta Winston, and Thelma Gruenbaum.

We would like to thank the editors of Austin Macauley Publishers for their assistance in having this book reach publication. The editors reviewed the manuscript and expressed a full understanding of the nature of the book and why it was written. In their acceptance letter they wrote: "We found the work charming and a heart-warming depiction of Beethoven's life. We found this title to be an engrossing story for young readers that will draw the audience into the unique story of Beethoven's life. Throughout the story, complex subjects – such as poverty and illness – are conveyed in a simple, easily understood way, yet without tempering the powerful message behind them. The overarching theme of resilience and overcoming hardship throughout the life experiences of this renowned figure is sure to inspire all readers."

Thank you to the illustration and design team for their excellent work.

The door flew open and David ran into the house. He dropped his sweater and schoolbooks on the table. "Mom," he called. "Tell me about Beethoven. The teacher said I should tell the class about him tomorrow."

Mother smiled as she hung up David's sweater. "Hello, David," she said. "You are very lucky today. Grandfather has come to visit us and he knows a lot about Beethoven. He often plays Beethoven's music on the piano. Why don't you ask Gramp to tell you about Beethoven while I go to the store?"

When David turned around, he saw that Gramp was sitting in a chair. "Oh hi, Gramp," he said. "I was hurrying so much I didn't see you. Will you tell me about Beethoven?"

Gramp smiled at David as he stood up. "Of course, I will," he said. "But first, if you like, I will play some of his music for you."

David clapped his hands. He loved to hear his grandfather play the piano. Gramp let him sit right on the piano bench so that he could watch Gramp's fingers.

Gramp opened a thick yellow music book and began to play. The high notes tinkled like bells. The low notes boomed like thunder.

David thought the music seemed sad and then it seemed happy.

Finally, Gramp stopped playing. "How did you like the music?" he asked.

David said, "I liked it. I wish I could play Beethoven's music."

"Maybe you can someday—if you work very hard," Gramp answered. "How long have you been taking piano lessons?"

David said, "One year. But I don't play as well as you do."

Gramp patted David's head. "It takes many years. It takes lots and lots of practice. You must play the same notes over and over again."

David frowned. "That's not fun!"

Gramp said, "It's hard work, but that is the only way to learn. You must practice until you are very tired. Then, just when you want to quit, you make yourself try it a few more times. And you'll find you can do it!"

"Is that the way Beethoven learned to play the piano?" asked David.

"Yes," said Gramp. "He worked very hard. His father taught him to play the piano when he was only four years old."

"Four years old?" cried David. "But he was just a baby!"

Gramp said, "Beethoven was very special. Probably when he was a little baby, he could sing back the tunes that other people sang to him. Most babies cannot do that. People said he had a very good 'ear'. I am sure that if someone played a note on the piano, Beethoven could tell you the name of the note."

"Oh, but that's so easy!" David laughed. "I can do that, too."

Gramp said, "Can you do it with your eyes closed, too?"

David looked surprised. "I sure can't do that," he said.

"Well, now," Gramp said. "Beethoven could. That's probably why his father began to give Beethoven piano lessons when he was only four years old. He knew that Beethoven was special—a musical genius. He was sure people would pay money to watch a small boy play the piano so well."

"What?" said David. "That sounds silly. Why would they pay to watch him play?"

"Beethoven lived some two hundred years ago," said Grandfather. There were no cars, mobile phones or internet then. There were very few pianos. People spent a lot of time listening to music at concerts. They were glad to pay money to listen to a child who could play the piano so well. Beethoven's family needed money. Beethoven had to practice the piano a lot so he would not make mistakes when he played for other people. He was only eight years old when he gave his first concert."

"I am eight years old, too," said David. "I make many mistakes when I play the piano. Tell me, what happened when Beethoven made mistakes?"

Gramp said, "His father did not like it when Beethoven made mistakes. He would scold or take away his supper. He made Beethoven practice many hours each day. Sometimes, he woke him up at night and gave him a lesson."

"Gee, I wouldn't like that!" David said. "No one takes away my supper when I make mistakes. I would not like to practice for hours. Why didn't he run away?"

"Maybe he felt like running away," said Gramp, "But he did not. He lived in the city, but he loved to run and play alone on the banks of the Rhine River whenever he could. He had happy dreams and thoughts then. He would forget how hard it was for him at home. He always felt happy when he was out of doors. He loved to hear the songs of the birds. When he was grown, many ideas for music came to him while he walked in the woods."

"Didn't he play with other kids?" David asked.

"Yes, he sometimes played with his two younger brothers and with the other children who lived nearby. But when he came home from school, he had very little time to play because he had to practice the piano. The neighbors often saw him crying as he played the piano," said Gramp.

"I would cry, too," said David. "A boy needs time to play games. He needs time to do what he likes."

"I am sure Beethoven felt the same way," said Gramp. "But he did what he was told to do. He loved to make up little songs of his own on the piano. But his father always made him practice things over and over again. I am sure he dreamed that someday he would do things his own way."

"And," said Gramp, "He finally did. But while he was still growing up, he had to work to earn money for his family. He went to school until he was 11 years old. He played the organ in the church. He took more lessons with other teachers. Finally, he had more time to write his own music. At first, he wrote music the same way that others before him wrote. He followed the rules of music. Everyone loved it. But Beethoven grew tired of that kind of music. He decided to change some of the rules because he wanted to try some new ideas. Some of the old rules did not make sense to him."

"Are rules like laws?" David wondered. "I mean, when you are young, you obey the laws. But when you grow up, you can try to change the laws if you think they are wrong."

"That's the idea," said Gramp.

"After Beethoven changed the rules for music, the music sounded different. At first people did not like the sound of his new music."

"Did Beethoven care that they did not like it?" David asked.

"Well," said Gramp, "I'm sure it hurt his feelings, but he knew in his heart that his music was right. He was not afraid to be different. Then, after a few years, people began to like his new music. Even the other musicians started to write new music, too. Beethoven was not afraid to be the first one to show them the way."

Gramp stood up. "I will let you hear some more of his music," he said. He picked up a large, flat square made of cardboard.

David ran to Gramp. "What is that?"

Gramp said, "It's a phonograph record." He tipped it sideways and a flat black disc slipped out. "Before the internet, it's how people used to listen to recorded music."

"Wait," David said. "What's that picture on the cardboard? Is that Beethoven?"

"Yes," Gramp replied, "that was what Beethoven looked like." Gramp handed the cover to David.

David looked at the picture and laughed. "He looks as if he never combed his hair!"

Gramp said, "Beethoven didn't care how he looked. He didn't care what clothes he wore. All he wanted to do was to write the most beautiful music he could."

"Didn't people laugh at the way he looked?" David asked.

"Sometimes they did," said Gramp. "But Beethoven worked so hard that he could play the piano better than anyone else. Then many rich people asked Beethoven to come live in their palaces. They didn't mind his funny clothes or the way he looked. He gave lessons to their children and played the piano for them."

David looked at the picture again. "He looks very sad. Wasn't he happy to live in a palace and play for the princes?"

Gramp said, "He could have made a lot of money playing for princes and giving lessons. But then there would be no time for writing music, which was what he wanted to do most of all. Often, he left the palaces and lived alone to write. Sometimes, when he needed money, he would go back to the palaces."

"But then something happened," continued Gramp. "He was sick. His ears started to buzz and hum. He went to many doctors, but they could not help him. Finally, when he was 28 years old, he became completely deaf!"

David covered his ears with his hands to see how it felt to be deaf. "What did he do?" he asked.

"Beethoven was afraid to tell anyone, even his friends, that he was deaf. He was afraid that people would not like his music if they knew that he couldn't hear. So, when people talked to him, he just walked away from them."

"I guess they thought he was rude," said David. "It's not polite to walk away when someone talks to you."

"That's right," said Gramp. "He needed his friends, but he made them angry. They did not know what was the matter. But he could not keep it a secret forever. When he tried to conduct the orchestra, everyone knew that something was wrong. Beethoven was so unhappy that he left the city and went to the country. He did not have to hear or talk there. He found it peaceful in the woods, and a wonderful place to write music."

"But I don't understand," David said. "How can someone write music if he can't hear?"

"A composer hears music in his own head," Gramp said. "He doesn't have to play the notes on the piano before he writes down the music. It is something like what you do when you read silently to yourself. When you look at a word in your book, you 'hear' it in your head even if you don't say it out loud. In that way Beethoven could 'hear' music in his own head even when he was deaf. But it is not as good as really hearing the music."

David clapped his hands. "I get it!" he cried. "But there is something else I want to know. When you played Beethoven's music for me on the piano, it sounded happy. If Beethoven was so sad, how was he able to write happy music?"

"Let me try to explain it to you," said Gramp.

"Beethoven felt a special way about life and about himself. He believed there is both good and bad in life. He felt that if you tried hard enough, you could make the good win over the bad.

"He also knew that he was a very special person. He believed that his music was a gift and he must find a way to give it to the world. There were many bad things in his life. He was sick and poor and deaf. It was not easy for him to write music. He had many reasons to be angry at the world. But he did not go out and smash things up even though he was very unhappy. Instead, he poured out his anger in the music. But this way he turned something ugly into something beautiful. So, you see, he made the good win over the bad. And his music shows the happiness and sadness he felt."

"Now let me ask you a question," Gramp went on. "What do you think happened when some princes came to Beethoven and said they would pay him well to write some music for them in the old style?"

"I bet Beethoven told them he would not do it!"

"You are right," Gramp said. "Beethoven needed the money, but he still said he wouldn't do it. He felt he should write music only the way his heart and mind told him to do it."

The door opened and there was Mother. "My goodness," she said, "Are you two still talking about Beethoven?"

"Gramp has told me a lot," David said. "Do you know that Beethoven had an awful life? He was poor and hungry. He had to work very hard when he was a little boy. But he was very good. He did not get angry and run away. And he didn't feel sorry for himself. Then, he became deaf, and he still wrote music!"

"Did he worry if people told him that they did not like his music?" Gramp asked David.

"No," said David. "He just wrote the best music he could. Later, the other people learned that it was good. Even when he needed money, he would not write music to please other people."

"I think you are beginning to understand Beethoven," Mother said.

"Yes," said David, "And I would like to hear some more of his music."

"Gramp can play some records for you," said Mother, "And then we can find some other books that you can read about him."

"A good idea," said Gramp. "We all know that Beethoven wrote wonderful music. You can tell that when you listen to it. But it is good to know something about his life, too. He was a very great man and he did not give up. From a sad and difficult life, he made something special—great music. The rest of the world has been enjoying it for over two hundred years."

CPSIA information can be obtained
at www.ICGtesting.com
Printed in the USA
BVHW020711060622
638960BV00024B/143